THE
PHOENIX
RISING

Mark De Klerk Buhler

ISBN: 978-1-63950-313-1 (sc)
ISBN: 978-1-63950-315-5 (hc)
ISBN: 978-1-63950-314-8 (e)

This publication contains the opinions and ideas of its author. It is intended to provide helpful and informative material on the subjects addressed in the publication. The author and publisher specifically disclaim all responsibility for any liability, loss, or risk, personal or otherwise, which is incurred as a consequence, directly or indirectly, of the use and application of any of the contents of this book.

Writers Apex

Gateway Towards Success

8063 MADISON AVE #1252
Indianapolis, IN 46227
+13176596889
www.writersapex.com

CONTENTS

The year Is 2185, one year after world War 3

In Mankind's fiery rebirth from the inferno of war.

INTRODUCTION OF OUR STORY

A traveler's spacecraft crew from Saturn's Moon Titan returning to Earth, After spending two years in Titan's orbit in conducting planetary / lunar research with there two stay on the moon and in its orbit there, has now come back home to soon a different Earth and will soon be landing on the earth's Moon deep space launch facility to find out that several weeks prior in the past there was a massive worldwide thermonuclear war destroying most of the northern planet on its land and parts of the oceans and its breathable atmosphere making it very uninhabitable to live and survive except for a few places in the south in Earth's southern parts.

The only hope for humankind to survive with remnants of bearable life are now living in the southern regions of Earth as in Australia, South Africa and on space stations, the moon, Mars and the Asteroid belt,

With now a small new laboratory outpost's here on Earth and in space for a beginning future for the human race is being experimented in a post nuclear war in its subterranean bases in Australia and South Africa to continue surviving on Earth and

+to continue exploring space and there future solar system quest and habitat and exploration has already begun, the year 2185.

Somewhere in space in the orbit of Saturn is the Marco Polo, Interstellar Spacecraft returning to Earth from the moon Titan..

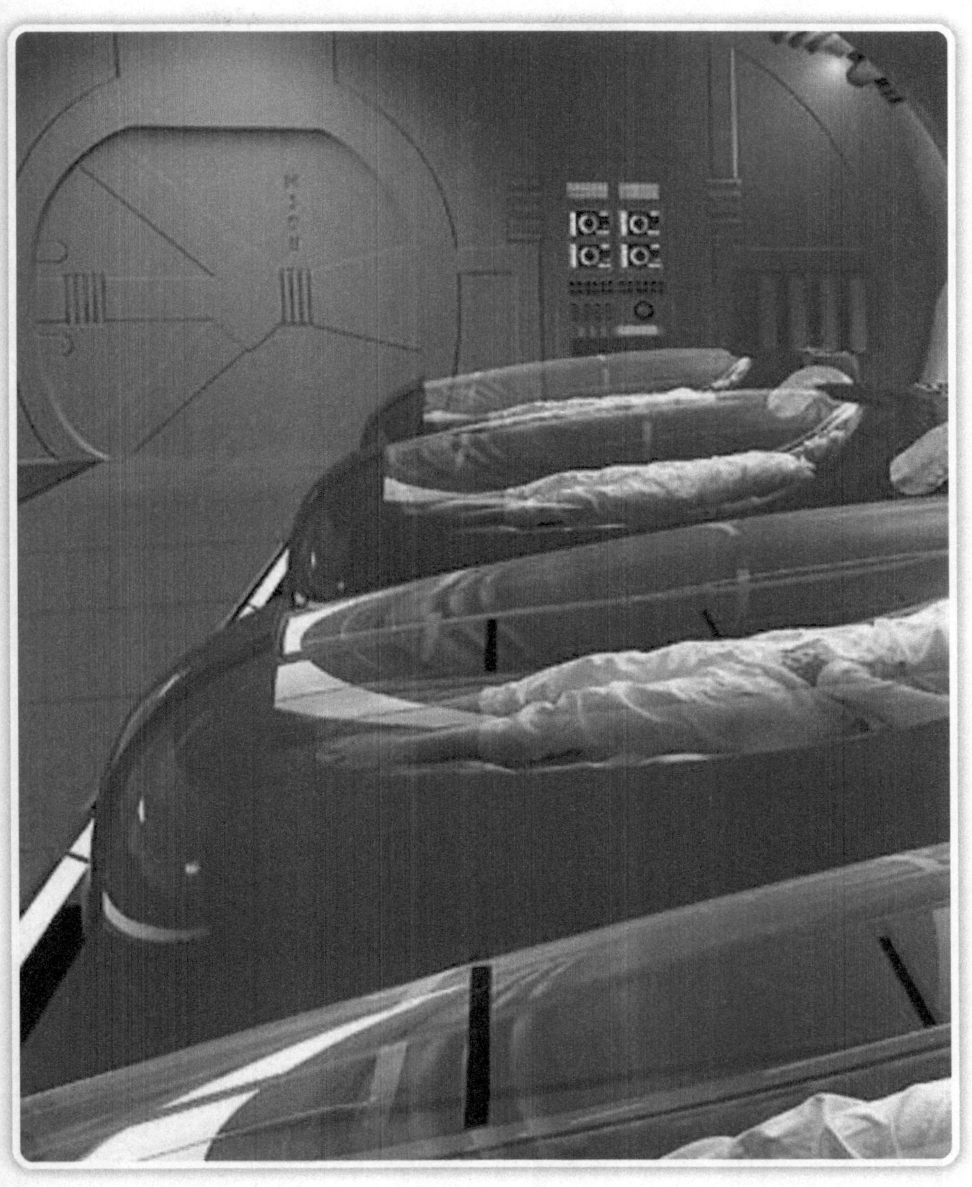

CHAPTER 1

EARTHBOUND TO A MASS KILLER

Space travelers returning from Saturn's titan moon are now coming out of a deep cryogenic stasis sleep, getting their life support going and doing a diagnostic of Marco Polo systems and final navigation settings to an Earth bound rendezvous with the 'Carl Sagan' space station and from there to an arrival at the Cape Canaveral landing pad No. 5. The crew is very excited with their treasure troves of data and scientific findings about the titan moon and also their findings of the ice-rock rings circling Saturn.

The space crew now are being contacted by the Earth's moon deep space complex facility, and finds out that world war III has just destroyed most of the human life on earth, we humans on the moon, mars and the asteroid belt will be in communication for mars to be the new capitol of a united off world human race to be stationed on mars in the near future. The seven astronauts will soon land at the copernicus natural vertical hole crater on the southern latitude deep inside the lunar entrance of the space launch and landing pad no. three spaceport and will go down below its surface to the commander and administrator Carl Higgins. In her space travel from Titan is the lead Commander spacecraft astronaut Ms. Anna Connors upon learning what has happened on Earth from the moons deep space ground communications center, that we cannot recommend you from transferring to an Earth shuttle now and you may have to go to mars for the rest of your life and your teams life, in never to return to Earth again, but for now you will be landing here on the moon's main launch pad.

Space Force Administrator Carl Higgins video-communications to lead astronaut Anna Connors, and said to her that one of the billionaires has sent one of his rockets to mars just last month containing 127 souls is now in deep space stasis and headed for a mars settlement landing in just two months time and we have also asked the orbiting space station commander to set also a course for mars, which this space station has this capability for space travel to do so.

With a space station population of 162 on board souls. Ms. Anna Connors said back to Administrator Higgins suggestion that there is no way we can let you go back to earth and he said no way and that the remainder population is way out of control where they will tear you to bits and with now the atmospheric levels of radiation in the high redzone of being lethal and you cannot I repeat, you cannot go back and land on Earth now perhaps in twenty years or so, a small expedition of helmeted astronaut scientist may go back there and find out the condition of the planet and perhaps seeing what we can ship back there to mars with anything useful for our needs and survival there on the red planet.

The moon's deep ground space center a mayday signal calling for help from an orbiting shuttle spaceflyer taxi needing whatever help you can give us and the moon's administrator Higgins said to the shuttle pilot of the dreamliner that there is no way we can help you now or never, you have to go back and land on Earth hoping you will survive somehow your outcome, the shuttle pilot said we cannot because radiation levels are becoming too lethal in earth's atmospheric world wide mounting deaths and we will simply be killing our two crew mates and seven passengers on board here. Listening in seven hours away in space is Commander Anna Connors now communicating with suspicion of why are you here in space orbit, with the two shuttle pilots, this is the spaceship, Marco-Polo, we can reach you in seven hours, by not going directly to the moon. The moon's Administrator Higgin said to Anna Connors do you have enough fuel and oxygen then to come here to our moon's facility and she said yes we do, then the Administrator Higgins said to her then go ahead and rescue them. Six hours later the Marco Polo has finally arrived and is now seeing the shuttle spaceflyer craft orbiting the planet and Anna Connors contacting the captain or pilot of the small dreamliner coming closer to the spaceship the dreamliner speaking with an arabic accent speaks to the commander of the Marco Polo and the co-pilot who speaks arabic as a second language with his fine tuned hearing begins to hear one of the people in the shuttle spaceflyer say once we get on board and we will take it over and kill these infidel morons,

the co-pilot tells captain conners what he has heard and she then stops the Marco Polo one thousand feet from the shuttle dreamliner and captain connors then says to their pilot we cannot take you aboard our ship and the shuttle pilot said to her what do you mean, the co-pilot in checks his instruments and notices a charged particle acceleration sensor within the shuttle dreamliner and captain connors then turns on her ship electromagnetic laser weapon slowly pulling back another one thousand feet from the orbital standing shuttle spaceflyer craft and ...

Then Captain Connors seeing on her instruments detect a coming full energy discharge, while the shuttle spaceflyer pilot says please come closer to us, and she said no, then the shuttle spaceflyer with no recourse, but has now discharged shuttles energy beam towards the Marco Polo, but just as the energy beam was about to hit the Marco Polo, Captain Connors put her port thruster on high in thrust turning the spacecraft around on its side and then nosed dived down thirty feet just missing the beam from the spaceflyer and then Captain Connors said to her co-pilot fire our laser weapon and he did just that, he fired the laser beam towards the spaceflyer striking it severely in damaging it in an explosive fire and then a fuller explosion coming only three seconds later destroying the shuttle spaceflyer completely, with Captain Connors saying to Administrator Higgins I had no choice, and now I am setting a course for the moon and the deep space facility.

Closing on to Earth's moon

As they were about to leave and head to the moon, the co-pilot instruments indicated a somewhat living person in a spacesuit speaking american asking for help, they then decided to move closer but stopping at five hundred feet from the space suited person from the Marco Polo they released a robot drone and sent it to the space suite where it picked up the individual detecting no explosives in the space suite with their senors and the robot came back to spacecraft and once inside they opened the space suit and on the lapel was a female individual that read a Dr. Maureen Tobey of Ceroma Industries, and now waking up looked at the seven crew persons and said to them thank you very much i was kidnapped and if i did not follow their orders they would kill me, and I did, and here I am with you, again thank you for my life, Captain Connors looking at her now smiling and said to the others i believe her to be okay, and now may I take your attache case from you and she said no, I need this for what's inside is top secret.

A life saving event ends well

The Marco Polo has now headed towards the moon with a strange guest and a puzzle about what has happened to Earth being destroyed in a thermonuclear war killing over ten billion people and what are we to do about the survival of the human race and for our future. It took a solid earth day to get to the southern lunar complex base on the moon where the spaceship Marco Polo landed on the lunar space launch elevator pad no. 3

now with the elevator taking them deep inside the reconstructed natural hole to sub lunar ground parking no. 5 and then the elevator moving sideways going horizontally inside to hanger 15 and then the eight people lead by Commander Connors went across a pressurised people transfer arm gateway to a second pressurized hatch door, going inside to the lunar deep space launch and tracking complex to see the lunar complex base administrator Carl Higgins.

In room 302 now waiting for them to arrive.When the astronauts and the one rescued scientist came inside the conference room, they all said hello to the Administrator Carl Higgins. With Higgins politely saying back to them hello and can you please sit down at this large circular conference table, I need to speak to all of you what just happened this past several days of world war three on earth.

Coming into the Oval Conference Room:

Marco Polo. spacecraft crew:

Ms Anna Magdalena Connors, Commander and Chief Pilot and advisor for planetary studies

Mr Gary Harmon, systems programming

Ms Lisa Thompson, VTOL robotic pilot engineer

Mr Thomas Watson, genetic bio-engineer

Ms Paula Carrington Reeds, Biochemist and food nutritionist

Mr Marc Conway, flight systems engineer, astronomer

Ms Eva Kerry, Marco Polo Co-Pilot, robotic engineer

And Ms, Maureen Tobey. Marco-Polo Navigation Officer

Theos-AI/5G Science and Engineering / Robotic Android, also known as 'Thera'.

And from the lunar command now sitting at the 0 table asking questions of the astronaut/scientists. In which there was inclusive answers given at this time.

<u>Lunar Deep Space Complex Facility Personnel</u>:

Administrator and General, Space Force, **Mr. Carl Higgins.l**

Marine colonel, **James Whitney Bowes,**

And Space Force lieutenant Colonel, **Susan Mcgovern.**

Air Force Captain, **Jennifer Richards,** computer programer.

Space Force Pilot, Lieutenant Colonel, **Maurice Cummings.**

Marine special forces.robotic ground vehicle controller, **Paul Redwood Stevens.**

U.S. Army Corp and Space Force member, Nuclear Medical Doctor, **Patricia Owens.**

<u>Also Included:</u>

Astrophysicist and British Stargazer, **James Gregory Wilson.**

With Billionaire Industrialist, **Dr. Leopold Henderson.**

And, Russian Nationalist President, **Mr. Yuri Antonov.**

And also, **Gerard Butler,** Space Force, Security Agent

Coming into the lunar oval conference room with Administrator Carl Higgins at the head sitting chair now presiding the meeting with the other eight people in providing them the background story of the events leading up to the nuclear war ending most of the human race on Earthl.

The end of most of the world

Administrator and General Carl Higgins said now sitting that one week ago Russia, Pakistan, China Iran and North Korea launched a world-wide thermal nuclear war against United Kingdom, France, India, Brazil, Israel, Japan and The United States declared war against each other as a result of the final ultimatum from nationalist madman Yuri Antonov of Russia in his last statement to the world in giving at the Geneva Conference for European peace at the Hotel Storchen, located at Weinplatz, 2-8001 Zurich, Switzerland

The nationalist dictator in telling the European leaders to surrender your countries to Mother Russia in twenty-four hours or we will declare war on Europe with each European leader saying no we will defy your commands and they told him we will never surrender to mother russia, and then in twenty five hours later russia launched its nuclear missiles at europe with two hundred divisions moving across eastern europe to not only occupying Berlin but to invade and attack Paris, France as well, and as a result Russia will declare war on any country defending and protecting Europe from total war in retaliation and in our nuclear inferno.

Administrator, Carl Higgins spoke further and said that nationalist madman dictator Yuri Antonov was not alone and except for India, all of Asia supported him launching their nuclear missiles not on Europe but on the United States of America which angry and was furious over russian european aggression and then it was all over with seven billion people who were dead with another one billion people dying of radiation poisoning, leaving the moon, mars and the astro-belt all alone to survive and to recreate the human race off of our home world, Earth.

Carl Higgins then said to the others present that I just spoke briefly with Scientist Ns. Maureen Tobey, and since she was present and endured the world-wide nuclear was she will first speak to you and how she was trapped and held by these terrorist who abducted the spaceflyer mini-shuttle craft. And now i want to give the floor to Ms. Maureen Tobey who will tell you who she is and a very interesting story that all of you will take part in the coming days to come now here she is please speak here Ms. Maureen Tobey.

Ms.Maureen Tobey speaking now tells the people here at the conference attending that I am chief scientist for my mentor and fellow scientist and industrial billionaire, Dr. Leopold Henderson the famed mechanical electronics engineer who has created in secret hiding a time machine with a capability to transport someone to one hundred years in the past or into the future. The time machine is located in a specialized underground installation located in the southern highland mountains of western bolivia in the Andes Mountain range. We at this underground facility finished our work and were just about to test the time machine when war broke out. We then had to move to our stasis chambers with a time set to wake us up in ten years time and then the one hundred and fifty personal then secured the facility to the outside preventing any nuclear radiation from penetrating and securing my fellow people.

Three of the people who claimed to be scientist stayed to the last moment with all of the workers in stasis holdings and then they pulled there guns on me and shot Dr. Leopold Henderson, and forced me to the underground space hanger of the modified dreamliner and with the one pilot just coming to the stasis chamber, commanded him and me to the spacecraft and we took off headed for the space station that was about to leave earth orbit for mars when your space ship came along and one of the terrorist said we will subdue the space travers and take over their spaceship for our own needs. Then your ship came and i had no choice but to leave the pilot of the dreamliner and with my spacesuit and extra small oxygen tanks and my small attache case on my belt when the chance came to leave with your beam assault hitting the spaceflyer I quickly opened the small back bay door and jumped just seconds before your beams destroyed the dreamliner and with my small thruster rockets made it it before the blast that would've killed me and then hoping my small communicator would reach your spaceship to pick me up and you did and here I am speaking to you now.

Then Carl Higgins interrupted Ms.Tobey and said to the people sitting around the conference table that as I speak to you now, one of our specialized and modified to a Long distance spaceflyer craft is being ready to take you if you volunteer for this mission to take you down to the Earth surface and land your team next to the mountain launchpad bay under ground facility and Ms.Tobey then will take you to a special hidden entrance way side the facility and she will help you activate your mission protocol assignment if you want to take it in exploring the remains of Earth.

Raising her hand Commander Anna Connors spoke to Higgins and Tobey and said we are a team here in spending several months time exploring Titans mysteries not knowing what but to explore this outer world for future settlement and human development. Coming now to Earth and seeing it destroyed makes us all sad and hoping we can somehow change our time-line and restore Earth as before will make us all very happy and Ms. Tobey agreed wholeheartedly with Ms. Conners.

Carl Higgins saying to all now sitting at this conference table here on the moon, if you have any questions for Ms. Tobey or me please ask them now and we will answer them for you at this situation conference table.

Person one:

Lisa Thompson

Question; nuclear war on earth?

Answer; we are monitoring the results there.closely.

Person two:

Ms Paula Carrington Reeds

Question;will I be going down to Earth.

Answer; no you will stay here onthe moon.

Person three:

Maurice Cummings

Question; will we be landing on the moon

Answer; yes that is the idea before we go to earth.

Person four:

Paul Redwood Stevens

Hello how are you,

Question; wil we be using ground robotics on earth.

Answer;yes you will with a short stay on the moon.

Loop

Person Five:

Patricia Owens

Hello how are you,

Question; will you need me on earth to help out.

Answer; yes you absolutely be needed with crew there.

Person Six;

Ms. Eva Kerry

Hello how are you,

Question; will I be needed on the marco polo.

Answer; no this time you will remain on the moon.

Person Seven;

Commander, Ms. Anna M. Connors

I Thank you for volunteering for this special assignment,

Question; thank you for the assignment

Answer; you are very welcome with your expertize.

Thera-AI/5G Robotic Android

I hope I can be your artificial intelligence aid on the planet to meet your science needs coming assignment. if not I will stay on the marco polo.

With all of your questions hopefully answered I as administrator of this lunar facility, i have the authority to identify and select eight people along with Ms. Tobey and commander Anna Connors, to go down to the Earth's surface in the modified transport spaceflyer going to this south american mountain site and enter the complex facility and select people to go back in time and change history by preventing nuclear war and allow the peaceful continuation of the altered timeline that will allow Earth to live on and to build the colonization of our solar system that has to continue for the benefit human history and adventure.

Administrator Higgins and Ms. Toby have asked the people sitting at the conference table to leave and rest and have a coffee break for one hour and then come back here and we will select the people to go down to the planet to the mountain site and they all got up and left. In the lunar facility mess hall cafeteria they all sat at the corner introducing themselves and telling each other what on Earth has lead to them to change the time and restore in an altered timeline that we will bring back life as we know it, and to go back to our routine personal life and home.

Administrator Carl Higgins has asked Commander Connors and the Android to stay with Ms. Tobey and myself and they all agreed while the rest went to the cafeteria mess hall with the four of them determining who should go and who will b left behind here at cornperticus. They all came back in from the cafeteria mess hall and immediately sat down, the Commander Anna Connors read the tablet list who stays and who goes back to Earth. She read the list names;

<u>Going to Earth, who will it be;</u>

Lisa Thompson
James Whitney Bowes
Maurice Cummings
Paul Redwood Stevens
Patricia Owens
Eva Kerry
Anna M Connors
And Thera-AI/5G Robotic Android

Thera AI/5G Robotic Android

<u>She also noted, not going; those who are not going to Earth who will it be;</u>

Thomas Watson

Paula Carrington Reeds

Susan Mcgovern

Jennifer Richards

Commander, Ms. Anna M. Connors stating that those not going will help Administrator Carl Higgins pack up and move to Mars and to the Elon Musk launch and planetary studies facility.

Ms. Anna Magdalena Connors
Commander of Marco Polo Interplanetary
Spaceship and Dr. Of Planetary (Outerworld)
studies and settlement development.

Then Commander Ms. Anna Connors saying to each of them staying it was nice knowing you and if we fail on Earth I will be joining you on Mars and thank you again. The eight remaining group going to Earth and Ms. Maureen Tobey who will guide us to the South American mountain facility will fill you in the do's and don'ts in your actions and procedures once you have entered the main space-time faculty.

Ms. Maureen Tobey who was holding tight and not giving up her attache satchel when she was rescued showed those who were going to Earth on the one hundred inch view screen behind administrator Higgins, Ms. Tobey continued showing the external and the internal mountain top schematics and pictures of what to expect when you get down there on the large heli-pad a half mile walk to the entrance which she shows those who are going which leads to the main hall and time machine apparatus, the power supply unit and the computers that will direct you to three months ago in zurich switzerland at the the Geneva Conference for European peace at the Hotel Storchen, located at Weinplatz, 2-8001 Zurich, Switzerland where the Nationalist Russian President, Mr. Yuri Antonov, will be speaking, and I am looking at you Mr. Paul Redwood Steven that you have only one minute to take your best shot or two and kill the russian president and then escape, once he is dead there will be another timeline and the Earth will be spared of nuclear war and when Commander Connors comes to Earth everything will be normal in this new timeline.

Administrator Higgins, interrupted Ms. Tobey in saying it is now 0700 am hours greenwich England maritime and everyone please synchronize your watches to go down at 0900 hours am to the level three launch platform pad tomorrow morning on the modified spaceflyer shuttle spacecraft to leave on your mission code named 'time restored' and now I will leave you and Commander Connors will be the lead pilot and commander of 'time restored' and she with Ms. Maureen Tobey will fill you in the details of your mission. I Thank you and good luck I will not be seeing you anymore and pease this is very important that you succeed in your mission and journey. They all stood up and thanked him and said back to him we will succeed in our mission and good luck to you also Administrator Higgins and good-bye.

It is 0900 hours am in the morning the next day at the lunar level three launch platform pad where they now all meet next to where they will be going into and boarding the modified dreamliner shuttle spacecraft that will take them to Earth orbit in approximately five hours time. The new commander of this specialized mission is Ms. Anna Connors who along with Ms. Maureen Tobey and Theos-AI/5G robotic android, will hand out there equipment and amory if needed at the mountain facility site and along with their tablets that will guide them through the facility handed out to them by Ms. Tobey.

Commander Ms. Anna Connors said to them do you have any questions now or any feelings about this mission that you may object to and they all said, no. And, then she said to them raise your hands and say all is missions go, and she said to them did you relieve yourselves in the restroom before coming here and they said yes, they all did that, and now she said please go aboard to your assigned seats and in thirty minutes time we lift off to Earth.

Commander Ms. Anna Connors, inside the cockpit sitting next to seasoned space and space force pilot Maurice Cummings are now waiting being transported to the lunar surface to be okayed for launch in fifteen minutes time with all systems ready a go for lift off. It is their lucky day all systems are operational by them and the flight systems AI Computer is in full agreement. Commander Connors has been given the go ahead to lift off in;

10, 09, 08, 07, 06, 05, 04, 03, 02, 01 and <u>we now have confirmed lift off.</u>

Now raising with there four main fiery hot thruster boosters they are ascending to one thousand feet, two thousand feet and then beyond to where they will circle the moon before navigating to the orbit of the Earth and then its landing.

Mean while under the five story surface dome lookout on sub-level one inside the lunar facility operations control room with several other scientist and space force personnel in sitting on one of the consoles desk is Administrator Carl Higgins contemplating the hopeful success of their mission with Astrophysicist James Gregory Wilson speaking to each other with Mr. Wilson in saying that what is now in real space time will not exist for they will create another alternate time sequence if they succeed where now in our space time there is only a fifty-fifty chance that they will succeed, Carl Higgins in looking at Mr. Wilson on the next console desk said to him that the odds of their success is better than that, and also in reply to Mr. Wilson said why do you say that, and Carl Higgins said that I know these people and their fortitude to win and that they will go down in securing their mission and that is why they will succeed, and Mr. Wilson looked and smiled back and said to Carl Higgins, that I am now hopeful of their success when they land on Earth.

In orbiting the moon they will check their in flight operational log with their computer and then confirm their flight plan with their navigation computer that all systems are a go, if not this will be the last time while in lunar orbit to abort their mission and then to return back to their launch space pad.

And, then securing everything is fine while in orbit of the moon with there navigation syschoration flight settings, checking in okay to leave the lunar surface in three minutes, now with each one on board looking out at Earth through their porthole windows in reflection, and after two lunar orbits they are now finally propelled with there high impulse cruising thrusters to their home world in five hours time, Earth.

CHAPTER 2

- -

AN AWAKEN TIMELINE

On there way to Earth, each one volunteer specialist were on there tablets with their assignments and procedures when they land at the heliport next to the mountain facility. The Marine, Paul Redwood Stevens noticed a special automated letter symbol on his top right of his tablet view screen, with an urgent look and see? It read and stated that your original assignment from Administrator Carl Higgins were for you to kill the russian president and now you will also kill the industrialist billionaire Dr. Leopold Henderson when you arrive three months in the past who will also attend the geneva science and peace convention three months in our past. Your mission is to end time machine manipulation and its horrible distortion of the timeline danger that it represents, if you have read this automated letter press yes on the button next to it and it will be erased, now please do so as no one will see it, please press and the Marine Steves did just that and his view screen went back to the group's mission statement thinking to himself I hopes this works or I will surely be killed attempting to change time and history.

It is now five hours later and Commander Connors has said to her co-pilot enter a wide orbit of Earth he said why I will show you and five minutes later they saw a special weapons based laser satellite in front of then automatically turning on and aiming for the spaceflyer, Ms. Maureen Tobey said to the commander enter these code numbers and it will kill and abort the laser from hitting us, she did that and Ms. Tobey also said to the Commander Conners now you have to turn off the automated turn on sequence and end its life for good. How do I accomplish that that, I am afraid you have to do a space walk by getting close to the satellite and entering these codes that I will transmit to your helmet view screen.

Then Commander Connors said of course I have to do a space walk. Then she went back inside of the spaceflyer shuttle and said to the others please put on your helmets and attach your bayonet oxygen hose to your starboard arm rest, they all did that now she attaches the life cord attachment to her belt and then she opens up the hatchback airlock door, and then she departs the spaceflyer and with her backpack thrusters she slowly goes fifty feet to the satellite console hatch and opens it up and reveals a touch screen and she touches it turning itself on and with the alphanumeric code given to her by Ms Maureen Tobey she enters the code on to the touch screen and then something horrible happened the satellite is completely on and aiming its laser to the spaceflyer.

The view screen timer reads 59 seconds for beam burst and now Commander Connors is becoming frantic in telling Ms. Tobey what should I now do, she said let me thing and now the timer reads 28 seconds and then Ms. Tobey said enter this code, that is all I can say to you, what is it Ms. Connors said back to her, she said to the commander enter this in caps, 'GINGER', she did that and at 3 seconds before the laser burst, the satellite is now turned off for good, and Commander Connors said to Ms. Tobey how did you know that, because that cat was his AI Robotic animal he created after the real animal cat got killed chasing a bird off the mountain cliff unable to find or save the cat, and Dr. Leopold Henderson said I will never have an alive cat again. Now Commander Connors very grateful came back inside the spaceflyer and the shuttle spaceflyer is now orbiting closer to Earth for an atmosphere braking and re-entry and will soon land at the helipad in the andes mountain facility.

The shuttle spaceflyer now slowly comes closer to Earth in its every orbit in getting warmer with its shielding, and with each orbit maneuvers it slowly goes towards south america just almost resting above bolivia and now Commander Connors says to everyone are you ready to land and they all said yes, and she said let's go for it, Our last orbit or revolution of earth will begin and we will now nose dive and enter the top layer of the ionosphere, and we will descend down until we reach the troposphere where we will release our four glide parachutes and retro-rockets is everybody in agreement they all said yes, again and here we go said Commander Connors and the spaceflyer went straight down into the ionosphere with the heat shielding measuring 4,600 degrees fahrenheit on the underbelly of the shuttle spaceflyer.

The trip down was wobbly moving left to right and was shaking everybody but only for a few minutes and then later on Commander Connors said to all the worst is now over and in two minutes we will release the four glide parachutes and in four minutes time the four retro-rockets and in five minutes we will land on the helipad and our destination near the mountain facility. As Commander Connors said, they all saw high above coming closer to the mountain tops of the Andes Mountains with Bolivia to the starboard right and Chile to the port side left. Then she initiated and engaged the retro-thrusters and braking the fall with everybody holding on and slightly nervous and after five minutes the spaceflyer slowly came down two miles per hour and finally with the wheel struts fully open to further the cushion, the landing the of the spaceflyer came to a complete stop on the helipad right in its center bulls eye and everybody smiled and congratulated Commander Connors and the pilot for a perfect landing while the four parachutes were also coming down on the mountain top near the spaceflyer and helipad.

They are now on radioactive Earth and looking out the port hole there were no flying birds at all. The passengers and crew suited up and digested radiation sickness pills and all of them fully loaded, they all were ready to move when Commander Connors opened the back hatch pressurized door and then they all left their safety of the dreamliner and went out and started to move toward the mountain facility a half mile away where seeing it walking closure they realized it is huge and after a fifteen minute walk they were on a terrace ledge and all of them looking straight down could see the floor below over three thousand feet down.

Then Ms. Maureen Tobey took out her touch screen tablet and aimed it at the very large folding door bridge and nothing happened, she tried again, with nothing happening and then again and someone in the group got an idea and took the tablet from Ms. Tobey and aimed the tablet closure to its base not falling off the terrace, and pressed it three times and it worked the sixty by twenty foot door opened in coming down like a drawbridge in medieval times and now fully opened and now rested on its terrace landing holder. The group raced and went inside only fifteen feet to a steel door with small blinking window and with the returned tablet, Ms. Tobet entered a code on the tablet and then the door opened up and before they moved beyond the door the group saw on the terrace five fully grown black leopard trying to cross the bridge and one of the group shot a few bullet rounds near them and they all started to leave with Ms. Tobey pressing the close key on the tablet and the door bridge rose and then closed with by now all the team group members went inside the second door way.

Moving inside the drawbridge leading tunnel to the well covered steel doorway they opened it and then walked two hundred feet and came upon an elevator where they all went inside and then Ms. Tobey pressed the main facility laboratory button and when they reached the laboratory and when the elevator door opened their it was then they were all impressed in seeing the time machine and its thorium reactor electricity batteries and command control consoles. Everyone is now seeing it except this one as they were leaving the elevator she saw on one button and it read the 'followers', Ms. Patricia Owens decided to go down to the follower labeled floor and see what is it all about and when the door opened she stepped out and saw row upon row of stasis chambers of people lying there in suspended animation she must have counted one thousand of these people and noticed something strange about them, they were all european white with blonde hair and blue eyes and all perfectly healthy without a single blemish on them, both men and women.

Commander Connors said to all where is Patricia Owens, we were supposed to stay together, I will attempt to reach her with my smart phone and walkie-talkie hybrid, I am calling you and where are you I am two floors down from you and I want to show all of you something, very well and they all went down two floors and when they came out of the elevator what they saw and felt was sheer disgust and why did your employer billionaire industrialist, Leopold Henderson do this Maureen Tobey and she said back to Commander Connors that we wanted to recreate a new benign being in a peaceful new world of one race for one race. They all looked at the individual stasis chambers and its medical regulatory food and medical console and then they heard a sound coming from the distant hallway coming louder and then looking at the new interlopers standing were seven robotic sentry soldier drones fully armed and ready to shoot them then our robot theos, said no and go away in the voice and dialect of Leopold Hendersons and they all left.

They instead decided to go back to the elevator two stories up and resume their mission and to put the marine staff sergeant. Paul Redwood Stevens back by three months before the nuclear world war destroying life on Earth was to begin. Back now at the time machine the robot android theos and the others started the procedure to start and to activate the thorium power generators and also to start the time machine in sending our marine sergeant stevens back by three months to the Geneva Conference for European peace and security, at the Hotel Storchen, located at Weinplatz, 2-8001 Zurich, Switzerland

After three hours they were meeting success in getting power not only online but syncing it to the power differential with the time dilation multi-coils of the time machine guidance computer and in less than one hour we will see if it works by sending this specialized small round sphere I am holding here said Commander Collins, and I know it will work because inside this small ball is a tracking and magnetic sensor device if it works our time machine console sensor will pick it up and will tell us in what year we send it too. Is everybody ready for a practice test, yes we are Commander Connors, well here we go, initialize the year three years ago on the helipad if it existed then we are a go with the marine, and are we ready yes we are, now please engage the time machine and Commander Collins then through the specialized small ball rolled it into the six multi-coils and then it disappeared without a trace on our timeline and in our console it read and appeared three years ago on the empty helipad with Ms. Maureen Tobey saying that Dr. Leopold Henderson was at that time in Zurich, Switzerland at the same science and peace conference.

Once successful with the small ball the Marine prepares for his time travel and Ms. Tobey gave him a special ring that he can come back with and with him is this large suitcase that is his small portable transport helicopter to the small town of Enchanta and from there to Paraguay and then fly a rented plane to Rio De janeiro, Brazil and from there to Zurich, Switzerland said Commander Connors and Maureen Tobey and Ms Tobey gave the Marine Sergeant Paul Redwood Stevens, ten thousand american dollars to pay your way there and here is your special case of your rifle, day scope and night scope and your your infrared range finder telescope for your successful missions end and also here I am giving you a special account and code to my special checking I have set up for you with over ten million american dollars, here for your personal use.

Now good luck and here you go in saying goodbye to you, and then the Marine Sergeant Paul Redwood Stevens,saying goodbye to all of the spaceflyer crew and Commander, Anna Connors, and I will be successful in my mission at the Geneva Conference for European peace and security at the Hotel Storchen, located at Weinplatz, 2-8001 Zurich, Switzerland, and now I will go inside the time machine six coils and Commander Connors then said to all to initialize and they said back to her, all systems are a go, and then Commander Connors said please engage, the time machine and their computer consoles says yes to do so, and now he enters completely the six coils length of the time machine walking right through the spectral time dilation screens and within a microsecond he disappears with no trace of him at all here in this mountain facility time period.

On top of and inside the mountain facility Captain Connors said to everyone what happened, we are still here and not on board the Marco Polo spacecraft coming to earth from space, Theo, the robot android surmised that Paul Redwood Stevens failed somehow in his mission in the past. Then Maureen Tobey said that I know these portable spacetime communicators and I will find out what happened to him, Then Ms. Tobey can you show me how to use these devices with the ring, and I will go instead of you to the past, then Commander Connors said to everyone that you will restart the time machine in five minutes, because I am going back two days before Staff sergeant Paul Redwood Stevens arrived on the helicopter pad and then made it to town, Ms. Connors said to Ms. obey I will need a satchel and small suitcase for my journey and she gave it to her, and I will stay at the small town's hotel for one night and then go directly to Zurich, Switzerland through Paraguay's hyperplane service to Europe..

In the meantime I will take this communicator devise and ring with me and for you Ms Tobey to keep in touch with me and then to synch the sub-channel communication with theo the android robot on a special frequency that has a tachyon time dilation receptor and I will then meet up with him in Europe at the conference science and security site.

The time machine to save humanity

Then she briefly stopping at the first steps on the floor that guides her to the past or to the future iris ray time beam leading to the space time dilation spectral apparatus in turning around to say goodbye to her and the spaceflyer crew, then she is waitimg for to be transported back into the past and she told her crew before leaving in one hour if something has happened to me, you then will go back to the shuttle spaceflyer and return to the moon, please I repeat again and give me one hour if you have not received my message through theos my communcator in not hearing from me at all then pack up and leave for the moon, and that's an order from your commander to you from me and they all understood and they all said yes we will do so, and now I say to you goodbye and and until somehow we meet again, good luck for now my team, please initialize and engage the spacetime device, I am now leaving you and then Commander Connors stepping on the floor tiles and engaging the apparatus time dilation machine on setting and then hearing the spacetime machine turn on sees and feels the beams emmiiers incircling around her and she is then zipped right into and through the special iris lens and then disappeared back three years ago on Earth.

Now at a different space time event in looking on her time wrist in her leaving somewhere, she then starts to check the stasis chamber at the life sign regulators on the spacecraft, and then resets their wake-up call, and to end their deep stasis sleep in three hours on the Marco Polo and then she is wisked away to go somewhere else, but where...?

Then back on Earth, with her communicator she contacts Dr. Henderson back three years ago, and then she summons their armed fifteen robots to apprehend the spaceflyer crew and take them to a special holding cell quarters, and then she engages rhe time machine and she automatically goes a few months into the future with pre-programed a special application routine to place her at a special location to meet with Dr. Henderson, and then she enters into the time dilation beam emitters by pressing her remote device button and now she is off to the past in going to the conference gathering site in Zurich Switzerland three years go.

CHAPTER 3

A TIME OF YOUR LIFE

It is three years ago just before the marine will arrive to perform his mission and now at the the Geneva Conference for European peace and security starting in a couple of days at the Hotel Storchen, located at Weinplatz, 2-8001 Zurich, Switzerland she walks up the steps into the grand lobby of the hotel and then going to the registration and reception desk is Ms. Anna Connors who speaks to the clerk and asks her if there are still any rooms available and she said yes I have one room that is free, but kind of small would you like it and Ms. Connors said yes, and then the clerk said how many days, and she said that would be five business days stay thank you very well said, Ms. Connors, your credit card has been approved, and here is your receipt and the clerk rang the bell for the bellhop clerk to come who will now escort you to your room.

After entering her room no. 723, with the bellhop putting her satchel and small suitcase on the bed, she thanked and then left now alone in the room she looks out the window and she has a nice view of the lake front row of boats and the street below with a view of the front hotel below, then she takes out from her bag in a secret pocket her small 9mm gun and timeline communicator, she contacts theo and tell the robot android do not mention this to Ms. Tobey but double check this date and in seeing how I and stevens were captured and warm at least five minutes before hand and theo complied and now I am signing off for now

Then she refreshed herself and went downstairs to the lobby and found her way to the conference room where the Russian President will attend and make his speech three days in the future.

While walking around the conference room she noticed a door with a good view of the stage and future lectern where the president will be speaking and with nobody watching she entered the doorway and it was a cleaning and broom closet, at the back of the closet was another door she opened it and there was a hallway leading one way to the kitchen and the other way to the loading dock. She walked towards the loading dock and she met one of the workers and said to him where do I go to the garage he said to her walk around the left loading dock go around to your left and walk straight ahead and there you will find the garage entryway, I thank you she said to him and then she went to the garage she then saw to her left before entering the garage, was the sliding door entryway to the two elevators and staircase to the hotel lobby. She went inside the garage and came out the auto entrance way leading to main street and the lake boat basin.

She then turned around went inside the hotel lobby and saw a sign, 'Tavern on the lake', and she went in to the bar and asked for a scotch and seltzer water, the bar maiden said we also have free barbeque chicken wings that are free to our guests here at the hotel, and she said make that a double scotch and a large seltzer water with ice and thank you, She got some barbeque chicken wings and took her scotch and water to an empty table for two near and in front of the television sitting down and watching the world wide news of the day. As she was eating her barbeque wings she gazed up to the television and there he was the Russian President, speaking in Moscow saying 'That our relations with europe is not going well and I will go in two days to Zurich, Switzerland and plead to the best of my ability for a sensible way out of europe's hostility towards my country.

I hope the leaders see it my way to strengthen peace at our borders. Looking at him she saw a nervous and agitated man looking for a conflict, but seeking a peaceful dialogue now only, but she knew he would step out of line and initiate a global world war in three month s time.

Commander Connors said to the bar maiden can I just have a little more of these delicious wings, the bar maiden said and I will bring it to you, please do not get up and the bar maiden gave her a nice portion of wings with handi wipes for her fingers and face.

Then guess who came on the TV screen, none other than Dr. Leopold Henderson, speaking of very soon a new and revolutionary discovery that our staff at Caroma Industries has just created changing life for everyone on this planet in a few short months and with our marketing campaign it will cost no less than $100,000.00 American Dollars for an adventure truly to satisfy the ticket holder that he or she will never forget. Commander Connors thought to herself what is he up to and why now is the Russian President going to initiate a world wide war.

She sat having her wings and double scotch whiskey and thinking intensely why are they doing this, both the russian looking on and Mr. Henderson with his time machine, with not his but the russian one thousand blond shock troops personally obeying the russian dictator taking over what is left of the world, and maybe transporting the russian blond men and women perhaps years into the future to escape the world wide radiations to subside and that will be normalized, for Earth to return back to normal with a new race, army and population with the russian madman nationalist as Czar of Earth.

Finishing her chicken wings and scotch she went up to her room and laid down to rest and one later her spacetime communicator came on and Ms. Tobey said to her that I just saw you and the marine in the stasis chamber, and Ms. Tobey said to her they must have secured you both and returned you two this timeline and put you into stasis, with hearing the incredible news of her future capture she ordered a strong cup of coffee from the kitchen and the robotic waitress server left and then she put an eye dropper and scooped up a small amount of coffee and with her mobile small chemical analyzer the machine read arsenic poison just enough to put her into a stupor sleep mode. She has now been notified that someone in this time period know she is here, and from now on she must be careful what she eats or drinks here, while waiting for the marine to show up.

She thought to herself I need some coffee and a sandwich and looking out the window she saw on the side street corner a cafe and said that is where I am going so walking out the hotel and down the street to the cafe she went in and sat down, then a waitress came along and she ordered from her a cheeseburger with sweet potato fries and a large coffee caramel latte, and while she was eating and enjoying her meal someone came into the cafe shop and looking at her, and she looking back to him and he said to her my name, Gerard Butler, here is my identification, and looking at it he said to her I am from Space Force security and as my ID states I am a colonel with investigations, kind of a spy, but more like an investigator, and I was sitting at the bar in the tavern having a cup of coffee and you walked in, I was realy and completely astounded you walked in and why you may ask, because just yesterday I left her from huntsville, alabama deep space training facility where in two months she will be rocketed to Titan from the moons new deep space launch pad. Commander Connors looking straight back to him said you may have made a mistake and then he from his pocket took out some receipts and transaction documents from South America, Paraguay, and landing here in Zurich at this hotel and guess what they are your accounts, passwords and the exact same signature of a Major, and new Commander of the Marco Polo spacecraft, and then she said back to him, why I guess you got me, so what are your plans for me, and he said nothing right now, but I will still be watching you very closely but in the event if you may need me here is my business card and cell number, I thank you Major, Anna Connors, I hope you have a nice day. Watching him leave the Cafe shop she thought to herself space force security and he believes that I am an imposter and from now on I must be very careful of being watched while I wait for the marine to come by at the hotel and in the meantime, calling the waitress over and asked her for a nice swiss made german chocolate cake.

That night she could not sleep and thought to herself perhaps a small nightcap of cognac might do the trick and then she got dressed and went down to the tavern bar and guess who was sitting there at the one corner of the bar, but my new friend Mr. Gerard Butler from Space Force Security, when I came in he saw me and I decided to join him, when I came to the bar he said to me what are you having, of course I said no, but he insisted so I said to him, coniac please and the evening bar maid gave me a nice cognac in its glass to me and I said to Mr. Butler, I thank you and then he said to me are you going to confess who you really are and why are you here now, as I was almost going to say to him why am I here, he interrupted me and do you see that gentleman and I say that loosely sitting at the other far end of the bar, she slowly turned around and saw him, and then I said to him who is he and he said back to me, that Ms. Connors is Russian Intelligence, GPU, she turned around slowly and saw him and said back to Mr. Butler, I am looking at him and he must be in his thirties and also he is blond, Mr. Butler said so, what, and I was almost going to tell him when at bar the Russian left his stool and went out of the tavern.

Then looking back at Mr. Gerard Butler, I said to him I am here on an assignment and I will meet tomorrow a gentleman that i intend to marry and not only that I have somehow a double in the states passing off that she is me, tomorrow after I meet my fiance we are going to the American Consulate and exposure as a fraud, he looked back at me and thought I was nuts okay if that's your story I will be seeing you around and good night Ms. Anna Connors until tomorrow, so he got up and left the tavern bar, and then she finished her cognac but just as she was about to leave coming into the tavern bar is Dr. Leopold Henderson and his assistant Dr. Maureen Tobey who went to a secluded booth just passing her from behind towards that corner booth, when they went to the booth to sit down she quickly left to go back to her room.

When she arrived on her floor room no. 723 she went in and sitting on her bed was a letter, she wondered who would send me a letter, well sh opened it and the letter said,

'Ms. Anna Connors of Space Force, you may not know me, but I certainly know you. Like you to come from the future to be exact three months in the future, where your

spaceflyer friends want to know what is happening with you, well tonight you are safe but tomorrow you and your military sergeant friend will be subdued and taken back to three months in the future as prisoners and put into the stasis chambers and then, well you and the sargents future won't be as promising or secure I guarantee you that, so please have a wonderful night sleep and tomorrow you and your military friend will join me into the future.

My signature, I will not sign but you will see me tomorrow, good night Ms. Connors'.

After reading the letter she took one hour before, she could finally rest and be able to sleep, she was thinking who could that someone be, I must know? but now I cant and who could that be? I must know, but I can't then she slowly falls asleep and the next thing she wakes up and it iis 7:00 AM the next morning and some time before noon she then immediately wakes up and runs to the shower because she knows that the sargent will arrive and find out what has happened to his mission. She quickly leaves the hotel and goes to the cafe and has breakfast of belgium waffles and german bratwurst sausage and plain coffee and the latet news tele-pad.

An hour passed by and she was finished very happy and satisfied and even not finishing her last coffee and paying her electronic tele-bill at the robotic cash register, then walks in gerard butler and then looking at him what are you doing here after my hangover last night and i am looking for a strong cup of coffee, *and you Ms. Connors, that I am going to treat you to a danish and a coffee of your choice, why are you doing this because I have to speak to you and there is a secluded bench across the road by the lake park, after she treated the space force security officer, they went to that bench and sat down, talking she said, will you please listen to me Mr. Butler, my name is Anna Connors and I am Commander of the Marco Polo spacecraft that came from Titan three years from now in the future, you look bewildered, let me explain further the reason why I am here is Dr. Leopold Henderson has another time machine in South America, in the Andes Mountains guarded by armed robots and he is playing with space time and he must be stopped for our future and the world's would you help me, and he said yes I will help you.*

Why am I here now is because in less than three months the Russian President is going to initiate a world war on Earth destroying everything including the spot you are sitting here now, while he is drinking his coffee and eating his danish and still looking bewildered, she continues, in approximately four hours from now my associate a narine shop shooter will come this hotel where the russian president will speak and kill him, preventing the russians from going ahead a declaring nuclear war. Mr. Gerard Butler said to and what is your game plan here, and she said to I am going to kill Dr. Leopold Henderson also, and then I will return back to the future, he said to me how are you going to that I have a ring tachyon device locked on me to every location to return to the future.

Mr. Butler said I am not sure but I will believe you and I am sending four security special agents here from Bonn European Space Council, American branch consulate, and they will be here in three hours, that is good said Ms. Connors, because I need you and your four security agents to help me, and he said we may not help you, but if the russian president were to die or Dr. Leopold Henderson also were to die we will arrest you immediately and your accomplice your Marine Sergeant Paul Redwood Stevens, your sharp shooter, fine I will take whatever help you may give me, and I have one question for you when we enter that hotel please watch very carefully for Ms. Maureen Tobey and Mr. Henderson, can you at least do that for me, and he said yes of course, and she said to him let us go we have a full day ahead, and he said back I will contact my four associates to join me at this hotel in three hours, she said to him and then we go down to the conference for science and world security beginning at 1:00 PM today and they left the park for the hotel.

Three hours went by and there was a knock at the door she opened the door and in coming to the room was Gerard Butler and four associates looking stone cold to me but this was not a social visit but the security and safety of the world. The five people questioning her about this absurd story and while they were talking she handed them the letter and then Gerard spoke, and the other special agents agreed, he said nobody is going to die today, I don't know whether to believe you or not but I told my associates to watch out for Dr. Henderson and Ms. Tobey, and she said thank you for assisting me, It is now twelve o'clock and Gerard said to his agents and Ms. Commander Connors let us go down to the conference room and be on the lookout for the marine sergeant and then they left and went to the elevator going down to the lobby and to the conference room,little did they realized the marine sergeant is already at the conference room but is situated on and inside the ceiling vent air conditioning unit and taking out his rifle and sniper scope sight he attaches them together and then he waits, and waits until 1:00 o'clock comes.

Conference of Death

The five agents and Ms. Connors, move from the lobby to the conference hallways to the conference room itself and so far they have not found the marine sergeant, and as they wait at the conference room is getting crowded with reporters and guests as well as russian security agents outside the conference room and inside. It is now five minutes before the Russian President arrives and as they wait a bell boy comes and delivers a letter to Ms. Connors, saying can you meet me at the hotel loading dock alone and she said to gerard I will be temporary leaving you, please wait for me and she left him and then as she was going to the hallway leading to the loading dock he said to his men follow me and they also went to the loading dock just in time as four hired thugs came out of a van trying to apprehend and take her away by force when the agents showed up they foiled the abduction and gerard securing Ms. Connors who said these are the hired association thugs sent by Dr. Leopold Henderson to kill you.

They then returned back to the conference room and Ms. Tobey looking at Ms. Connors bewildered like you are still here and Ms. Connors finally realizing that Ms. Tobey sent me the letter and both she and Dr. Henderson looking at me decided to exit the conference room and gerard said to the four agents follow them, while I and Ms. Connors stay here, the special agents left and now comes the russian president coming into the conference room and going up to the stage and to the lectern podium and speaking about what he believes is a european betrayal in not including russia in international affairs and allowing the stationing of military troops at near the border, and in not signing a peace agreement for increased trade and scientific cooperation and doing this at russia's expense and security and I want to know why...?

He went further if europe were to understand russian concerns and needs we would understand and then speaking to reporters and even guests attending there was a sudden shock and sound of three shots being fired from above in the ceiling air conditioning vent that is big enough for a small person with a sniper rifle, and the russian president laying on the floor was pronounced dead with the vice premier coming to the lectern and sadly announcing to everyone the demise of President Yuri Antonov with Gerard and Ms. Connors looking horrified and then suddenly leaving to find the marine sergeant with his rifle warm, before he activates his time ring, escaping then leaping into the future.

Space force security special agent, Gerard, said to Ms. Connors, I am going to the garage and around the loading dock and you stay here and look for him at the lobby and contact me on your smart communicator phone. Then he left to go to the garage in back leaving Ms. Connors alone then immediately she went up to her room where she enters coming in sees the marine sergeant waiting for her and the two of them turning on their portable space time dilation ring device they dematerialize in this time zone and are propelled three years into the future at the South American mountain facility coming upon the helipad and the spaceflyer now parked and then running to the upright drawbridge and then Commander Connors, then talking quickly with the Sergeant, Paul Redwood Stevens, they both now see the drawbridge open and now slowly coming down and then she said follow me and he did and they quickly went to the helipad and parked spaceflyer and said follow me behind those bushes and lock and load and I hope we do not use them, let us kneel and hide behind the bushes here, and now waiting patiently they see not their crew members coming, but Dr. Leopold Henderson, and his assistant Ms. Maureen Tobey reaching for the spaceflyer.

Then Ms. Connors said to the marine let's go guns showing, they come out of the bushes and reaching the two of them at the spaceflyer, Ms. Connors said to them go and lye down on the ground or we will shoot you, they reluctantly did that and with rope secured them to the wheel struts of the spaceflyer, and then running to the drawbridge and into the holding cell where the rest of the crew were glad to see them and releasing their crew mates, and before leaving Ms. Connors checked the stasis chambers and found them all empty with no signs of them and it is her belief that they were sent into the future to where she does not know,

Then leaving the mountain facility with her crew mates across the drawbridge and walking to the spaceflyer they saw securely tied the two criminals, and then Ms. Anna Connors saw in the distance a large transport helicopter coming to them and landing next to the spaceflyer and out of the helicopter came Gerard Butler with twelve special space force agents.

Coming to the spaceflyer her crew mates and the two sitting grounded waiting criminals looking at the special agent, and then Ms. Connors said I am glad to see you Gerard Butler once again after almost three months and he said likewise I am glad to see you, and I see you got my note on the bed in telling you were I will be right now and he said to me yes I did and here we are that these two criminals apprehended will go away for a long time and as for those blond men and women conspirators, she said I believe Dr. Leopold Henderson and his accomplis Ms.Maureen Tobey took care of them for they have left for the future and later I will show you the other facility where this, other time machine must be destroyed, and telling her crew mates we will soon go to the moon. With the two of the special agents keeping them guarded so no harm will come to them.

Gerard Butler said to her that's why we are here and in our helicopter there is enough explosives to destroy this mountain facility and the time machine, forever and looking at the time marine the sergeant then said to her and him, I did not see you here, and they thanked the sargent for not arresting them, because he said we did not find or arrest the killers on a world view screen telephone communication kiosk by them to the new president of Russia, with the new Russian President, Nikovy Pavloff saying one day we will.

Later that day on world television,the new president, Pavloff 'has been appointed from his earlier post as an Agricultural Minister who favors peace and dialogue with the west, as the new president of his country and will help the Americans to find the killers of our former and beloved assassinated president.

Gerard looking at the world television, says the killers have completely disappeared and is not to be found for now. Then hearing and looking up in the near distance is another helicopter now coming this time with these captured criminals being escorted by police officials to take these found hiding criminals to Santiago, Chile lock up jail, and then later to be extradited to an American prison for a lifetime sentence.

With the altered second timeline restored we are now said Conners that a tyrant will never come again on our planet, Earth, now she is looking up at this city having a cup of coffee and a sweet cake seeing the restored cities skyline and the roar of the traffic go by, with her smiling of a peaceful world in which she will always call home.

Now what is your plan to from here on Ms. Commander Connors, we (my crew) will be taking off for the moon, but only for one month and then spend six months on Mars at the Elon Musk advanced studies on outerworld studies of Triton and Pluto, and then return to Earth and head to Washington D.C. to plead for more funding,, and you Mr. Gerard Butler I will be in Washington also in eight months and then head to Ceres and I hope to see you in eight months in Washington DC there, she said I hope so and now we have to go now and watching her crew board the spaceflyer he waved to her and she waved back to him and then the spaceflyer lifted off then slowly in gaining speed as they now go beyond the ionosphere into space and towards the moon complex base with lift off for their planetary and moon destinations, and for Ms. Anna M. Connors in the near future returning to Earth at Australia's new sub-desert Dundee underground Earth facility survival base for any uncertain future and life that may happen there next, but that today she said, the world is not at war with itself and that is a great thing for our peace and interplanetary exploration.

The End of my story,
The Phoenix Rising.

Author and writer, Mark Deklerk Buhler

THE PHOENIX RISING, BIOGRAPHY

In 2185 a Euro-Asian mad man initiated world war 3 in Europe, America, and Japan. And with his Asian allies launching missiles, killing over ten billion of the world's population and destroying its many buildings and infrastructures, this is now the end of mankind for the people of Earth.

In a far away mission to titan orbiting Saturn is a heroin who may reverse the worldwide calamity by our heroin going back in time, and killing this despot in his timeline will now be the only way for peace and our future to occur.

Our heroin is named. Commander Anna Magdalena Connors, who is now our only hope in saving the world and if she fails in her quest for the survival of mankind, all of space exploration and earth's future will be lost to whatever mankind hopelessly does to resurrect itself for the next one hundred year's, will she save mankind and create a new timeline future....?